MW01516863

Sir Rhymesalot

Dustin Dog Hair

Blues Hound, on the wrong side of town

Sir Rhymesalot

This book contains rhyming Tools. Scan the QR code to find out how they work.

FLOWCODE

PRIVACY.FLOWCODE.COM

When Dustin woke
up this morning,
He heard a
disturbing **sound**

He searched all over
his dog house,
But he just couldn't
sniff that sound **down**

When Dustin hit the streets,
it was almost a quarter to **nine**
He had to track down, that curious sound,
that was driving him out of his **mind**

Well the city is loud, rude and **scary**
And often can get a bit **hairy**
Dustin was tough but he'd had quite enough
Of this bone that he just couldn't **bury**

The sky was getting dark
When he crossed the railway **tracks**
As the night got later,
that big interstater,
wound its way to Clackety **Clack**

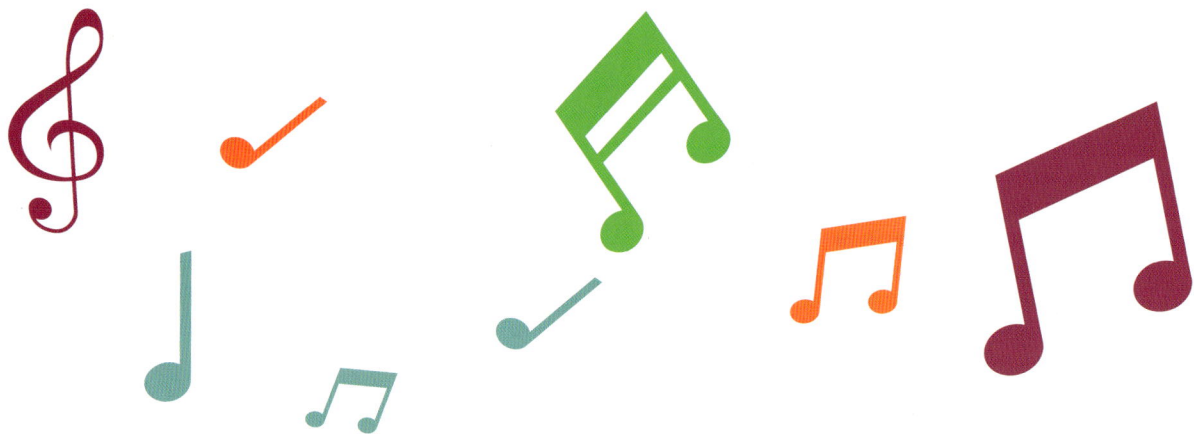

Dustin was getting jumpy
He was a hound on the wrong side of **town**
But what happened next,
had him somewhat perplexed
The source of the sound had been **found**

He was frozen right there in his **tracks**
Surrounded by fat hairy **rats**
But Dustin was determined,
To get past the vermin
And somehow attempt to get **back**

You could have heard a pin **drop**
The tormenting noise had now **stopped**
There in front of Dustin,
was a sight quite disgustin'
A four-piece rat pack looking **shocked**

"Ever since the day I was born,"
he cried,
"My father and mother were **proud**
But we were quite poor
And we lived right next door
To a rat band that played very **loud"**

"Now the Doghairs are quite slow to anger
And we remain calm around danger
But one thing makes us lose it,
That's Gangsta Rat Music
And the golden–toothed Gansta–Rat crowd"

Well the rats were very **offended**
They thought their rat music was **splendid**
But no need for alarm,
they used their rat charm,
and invited Dustin to **bend it**

So Dustin picked up his **Axe**
And started to jam with those **rats**
And the next thing we knew,
They were playin' rat blues
Backed up by a choir of **cats**

So should you be out in the **city**
Alone in the alleys a–**gritty**
You might hear the sounds
And the grooves layin' down
To miss it would be such a **pity**

And Dustin decided to **stay**
He still hangs with the rat pack to **play**
It just goes to show,
you can never quite know
where your journey might lead you **today**

When Dustin woke up this morning
He heard a disturbing **sound**
But as the day ended,
he was newly befriended
and they all broke some barriers **down**

Scan this QR code with your phone camera for more titles from imagine and wonder

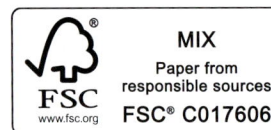

PRINTED WITH SOY INK ™
Trademark of American Soybean Association

FLOWCODE
PRIVACY.FLOWCODE.COM

FSC
www.fsc.org
MIX
Paper from responsible sources
FSC® C017606

Your guarantee of quality

As publishers, we strive to produce every book to the highest commercial standards. The printing and binding have been planned to ensure a sturdy, attractive publication which should give years of enjoyment. If your copy fails to meet our high standards, please inform us and we will gladly replace it. admin@imagineandwonder.com

IMAGINE & WONDER ™
Publishers, New York

© Copyright 2021 Imagine & Wonder Publishers, New York
All rights reserved. www.imagineandwonder.com
ISBN: 9781953652577 (Hardcover)
Library of Congress Control Number: 2021933825

Printed in China by Hung Hing Off-set Printing Co. Ltd.

Scan the QR code to find other
Sir Rhymesalot books and more from
www.ImagineAndWonder.com